Jeremy Strong once worked in a bakery, putting the jam into three thousand doughnuts every night. Now he puts the jam in stories instead, which he finds much more exciting. At the age of three, he fell out of a first-floor bedroom window and landed on his head. His mother says that this damaged him for the rest of his life and refuses to take any responsibility. He loves writing stories because he says it is 'the only way you alone have complete control and can make anything happen'. His ambition is to make you laugh (or at least snuffle). Jeremy Strong lives near Bath with his wife, Gillie, three cats and a flying cow.

www.jeremystrong.co.uk

ARE YOU FEELING SILLY ENOUGH TO READ MORE?

THE BEAK SPEAKS
BEWARE! KILLER TOMATOES
CHICKEN SCHOOL
DINOSAUR POX
GIANT JIM AND THE HURRICANE
KRAZY COW SAVES THE WORLD – WELL, ALMOST
THERE'S A PHARAOH IN OUR BATH!

JEREMY STRONG'S LAUGH-YOUR-SOCKS-OFF JOKE BOOK
JEREMY STRONG'S LAUGH-YOUR-SOCKS-OFF EVEN MORE JOKE BOOK

The Hundred-Mile-An-Hour Dog series
THE HUNDRED-MILE-AN-HOUR DOG
CHRISTMAS CHAOS FOR THE HUNDRED-MILE-AN-HOUR DOG
LOST! THE HUNDRED-MILE-AN-HOUR DOG
THE HUNDRED-MILE-AN-HOUR DOG GOES FOR GOLD

My Brother's Famous Bottom series
MY BROTHER'S FAMOUS BOTTOM
MY BROTHER'S HOT CROSS BOTTOM
MY BROTHER'S FAMOUS BOTTOM GETS PINCHED
MY BROTHER'S FAMOUS BOTTOM GOES CAMPING

THE KING OF COMEDY

Jeremy STRONG

KIDNAPPED!
The Hundred-Mile-An-Hour Dog's Sizzling Summer

Illustrated by Rowan Clifford

PUFFIN

PUFFIN BOOKS

Published by the Penguin Group
Penguin Books Ltd, 80 Strand, London WC2R 0RL, England
Penguin Group (USA) Inc., 375 Hudson Street, New York, New York 10014, USA
Penguin Group (Canada), 90 Eglinton Avenue East, Suite 700, Toronto, Ontario, Canada M4P 2Y3
(a division of Pearson Penguin Canada Inc.)
Penguin Ireland, 25 St Stephen's Green, Dublin 2, Ireland (a division of Penguin Books Ltd)
Penguin Group (Australia), 707 Collins Street, Melbourne, Victoria 3008, Australia
(a division of Pearson Australia Group Pty Ltd)
Penguin Books India Pvt Ltd, 11 Community Centre, Panchsheel Park, New Delhi – 110 017, India
Penguin Group (NZ), 67 Apollo Drive, Rosedale, Auckland 0632, New Zealand
(a division of Pearson New Zealand Ltd)
Penguin Books (South Africa) (Pty) Ltd, Block D, Rosebank Office Park, 181 Jan Smuts Avenue, Parktown
North, Gauteng 2193, South Africa

Penguin Books Ltd, Registered Offices: 80 Strand, London WC2R 0RL, England

puffinbooks.com

First published 2014
003

Text copyright © Jeremy Strong, 2014
Illustrations copyright © Rowan Clifford, 2014
All rights reserved

The moral right of the author and illustrator has been asserted

Set in Baskerville MT
Printed in Great Britain by Clays Ltd, St Ives plc

British Library Cataloguing in Publication Data
A CIP catalogue record for this book is available from the British Library

ISBN: 978-0-141-34419-5

www.greenpenguin.co.uk

MIX
Paper from
responsible sources
FSC
www.fsc.org   FSC® C018179

Penguin Books is committed to a sustainable
future for our business, our readers and our
planet. This book is made from paper certified
by the Forest Stewardship Council.

This is my hundredth book and I think it's a
good time to thank all the animals that have been
a constant source of inspiration and comfort,
namely our pets – mine and yours! Here are just
a few of mine that need a special mention:
Lucy, Tau, Machiavelli, Rubbish,
Bandit and, of course, Jeeves.

Contents

1 Jabbed with the Eiffel Tower

You can't blame me. All I did was jump out of
the window. OK, so it was the big window at the
vet's surgery. Mrs Vet-Person shouldn't have left
it open, should she, and anyhow, what would you
do if a vet came at you with
a whopping great big
needle?

'Just a tiny jab,'
Mrs Vet-Person said.
Oh yes? I saw the evil
grin on her face AND
I saw the size of the
pointy needle. Big? It
looked like the Eiffel
Tower! I was off like
a streak of lightning.

(No, actually, I was off like a Streaker because that is my name – Streaker – and I am the speediest speedster in the World of Dog-Speed.)

I saw the vet, I saw the needle and I saw the open window. *SWOOOOOSH!* I was gone in a flish-flash! Ha ha! You can stick that needle in someone else's bottom, Mrs Vet-Person!

They all came chasing after me of course, but I was way too fast for them. Those two-legs

can't run properly at all. I keep barking at them.
'Use all four legs! You can't run properly on
two! You've got to use all four legs, like me!' But
they never hear. That's because they have very
small ears, unlike mine, which go flip-flap like
towels on a washing line. I can catch the teeny-
tiniest sounds, even like an ant sneezing or an
earwig with earache going 'Ooooh!' in a very small
earwiggy voice like that.

Of course I was in big trouble at home after I'd run away from Mrs Vet-Person. Even Trevor Two-Legs, the boy I have to take for walks, was fed up. I thought he'd be pleased at my nifty bit of escapery but he wasn't. He was upset.

'It's for your own good, Streaker,' he told me.

Oh, really? My own good? I don't think so! I said, 'I'd like to see you get vaccinated with the Eiffel Tower!' Of course he didn't understand a word I said. Humans are hopeless. What's the point in having a dog as a pet if you can't understand what it tells you?

I had a long chat with Erik the Cat about it after I'd got home.

'Of course,' Erik said to me as he lay across half the sofa the way cats do. 'You do realize that you won't be going on holiday with them?'

'What holiday? What do you mean?'

'If you ever paid any attention to the two-legs, instead of living in a dreamworld made of sausages and pies, you would know that they are going on holiday in a few weeks, to France.'

A dreamworld of sausages and pies? I don't think so! Sausages and pies are VERY REAL and IMPORTANT! Plus, if I was about to go on holiday I would need a suitcase full of them, unless the place we were going to had plenty. So I asked Erik.

'France? What's that?'

'It's another country,' sighed Erik. 'Sometimes I wonder about your education. Don't you know anything?'

'I know lots and lots,' I told him. 'But I don't know about France. Can you eat it?'

'No. It won't fit in your mouth.' Erik smiled. I think that was meant to be a joke but only he understood it. I was still in Mystery-land.

'It's another country on the other side of the sea. Two-legs go there for holidays. Sometimes they take their pets with them. Your pal Trevor wants to take you, but they won't let you into France unless you have had your vaccination.'

I looked at Erik. My legs were going wobbly. 'You mean that thing like the Eiffel Tower?'

'Oh, do stop being such a drama queen,' sighed Erik. 'It's just a tiny jab.'

'That's what the vet said,' I muttered.

'Do you want to go on holiday to France, or not?'

'Is France nice? Do they have dogs there?'

Erik groaned loudly. 'There are dogs everywhere, numbskull.'

'Even on the moon?' I asked, wide-eyed.

'Only you would ask a question like that,' sighed Erik again. 'Of course there aren't any dogs on the moon.'

'But you said they were everywhere, so numbskull yourself. *Nurr!*' Ha! I'd caught Erik out all right, pretending he was so clever. That moggy didn't know much at all. I knew there were no dogs on the moon. I was just checking.

Anyhow, that conversation made me think. The two-legs were going on holiday and wanted to take me with them but I couldn't go unless, unless – *woofy-aaaargh!* – the Eiffel Tower!

No wonder Trevor had been upset. I was going to miss out on a holiday with him. But what sort of holiday? I would have to be a doggy detective and find out, so I followed them around with my ears going flip-flap in case I caught a clue or two.

It turned out that Mr Trevor's dad wanted to play golf. In France. I don't know why he likes golf so much. Those white balls are horrible – and I should know because I ate one once.

CRUNCH CRUNCH! It's like chewing a whole pile of rubber worms. **YUK!** I had to spit it out. **SPLURRGH! SPLURRGH!**

Anyhow, Mr Trevor's dad had booked a camping holiday near a golf course in France. (France doesn't just have dogs, it also has golf courses.) But Mrs Trevor's mum said she hated golf and she hated poky tents even more and she'd rather stay in a beehive. (Is she *nuts*?????? I shall never understand those two-legs.)

Then Trevor said golf was the most boring game in the world and Mr Trevor's dad went red and began spluttering all over the place and marching about the room waving his arms around like a policeman directing the traffic only there weren't any cars, just a sofa and two armchairs – and they weren't even moving.

Mr Trevor's dad was trying to tell them that the campsite didn't just have golf nearby, it had mountain biking and archery and rock climbing and paintballing and canoeing and they wouldn't be in a tent at all because he had hired a caravan. A special silver caravan.

That was when they all went bonkers. Actually, first of all there was a long silence while they all looked at each other and Mr Trevor's mum said 'Mountain bikes?' in a kind of squeaky excited voice and Trevor said 'Canoeing?' in an even more squeaky excited voice and Mr Trevor's dad said 'Yes.' Then they began shouting and screaming and bouncing around like three ice creams that had just won first prize in an ice-cream-on-a-trampoline show.

When they had stopped being ice creams
Trevor went all quiet and said he couldn't go on
holiday unless Streaker was with them. (That's
me, Streaker! As you can imagine my ears
REALLY pricked up at that point. In fact my
ears stood up like rockets on take-off.)

Mr Trevor's dad didn't seem very happy
about me going on holiday with them. In the

end, though, they decided that Erik could stay behind and be looked after by a cat-sitter but they couldn't leave me because I was unreliable. I have no idea what 'unreliable' means but it must mean I am something very special and precious otherwise they wouldn't be taking me on holiday, would they? Anyhow, to go on holiday I need a rabies vaccination.

'I don't see the point,' muttered Mr Trevor's dad. 'Streaker behaves as if she's already got rabies.' And they all laughed. I asked Erik what was so funny but he was laughing so much he fell off the sofa. Serves him right too.

Eventually he told me.

'Rabies is a disease that makes you froth at the mouth and snarl a lot and it looks like you've eaten a bar of soap. In fact you go mad. And then you die.'

'I'm not mad,' I said. Erik just looked at me. 'I'm not,' I repeated.

'You jumped out of the vet's window,' Erik pointed out, 'and last week, you ate a cushion because it had a picture of a burger on it. You're completely insane.'

Huh. Erik can be so . . . catty. I went up to Trevor's room. He was lying on his bed looking sad so I lay on his bed and looked sad too. Then I realized he couldn't see me looking sad because I was lying on his head and in any case he was

waving his arms about because he couldn't
breathe, so I got up and rested my head on his
stomach and said I was sorry and I'd go to see
Mrs Vet-Person with him if he really wanted.

I said all that without even moving my lips.
I did it with sign language, using my ears. I'm
pretty good at that and Trevor is clever so he
knew what I was telling him.

He looked me in the eyes and nodded.
'Tomorrow, then. Tomorrow.'

So that's it. Tomorrow I'm going to have the
Eiffel Tower stuck in me.

2 An Awful Lot of Fuss Goes On

I'VE DONE IT! I've been vaccinated! It was easy-peasy. I didn't feel a thing! I went with Trevor and he gave me three jam doughnuts and by the time I'd finished eating them Mrs Vet-Person had done it and I didn't even notice. I don't know why Erik made all that fuss about it.

There was lots more fuss today because first of all we had to go off to this funny box kind of place and Trevor tried to get me to sit on a seat, which was impossible because the silly seat was only just the size of my bottom but there was still the rest of me, wasn't there, like my stomach and legs and stuff and where was all that lot supposed to go?

'Just sit up,' Trevor kept telling me. 'Stop moving and keep still. KEEP STILL!'

How was I supposed to keep still when my legs kept falling off my seat? Then my legs would pull my tummy off because they were all joined together and my tummy was joined to my neck and head and then they were dragged off until eventually all of me was on the floor. Again.

Mr Trevor's mum was there and she spent most of the time leaning against the box thingy and having hysterics. Eventually Trevor got under the seat and held as many of my bits up as he could while the machine went flash-flash at me and made me blind. We had to wait

after that until something came out of a little slit in the side of the box and I thought it was chocolate like you get from a chocolate machine at the station so I ate it.

Guess what? It wasn't chocolate. It was some horrible glossy thick paper thing that tasted like someone's sick so I spat it out. ***SPLURRGH!*** Then I was in trouble because apparently they were the photographs for my passport so we had to do the whole thing all over again.

Now I have my own
passport and it's got a
picture of me on it looking
smart except that my
mouth and jaw have gone
wonky and my tongue's

sticking out. That was because Trevor's hand
was holding my muzzle very still while the photo
was taken. Trevor's hand is in the picture too so I
guess the customs control people will let Trevor's
hand come on holiday with me because it's in the
photo but I don't know about the rest of him. I
hope that can come too.

When we got home Mr Trevor's dad laughed
at my picture and so did everyone else, including
Erik. I don't know why but most people seem to
either laugh at me, or yell. Or both. Well, I'll tell
you something about Erik that will wipe the smile
off his face. Do you know what his real name is?
The family call him Cutie-Pops. Ha ha! Cutie-
Pops. Is that a respectable name for anything?

I don't think so. I wouldn't even call a tadpole Cutie-Pops. (I'd call it Froglet, which is like a frog, but smaller. Or Tiddles.)

Anyhow, Mr Trevor's dad had something to say to Trevor. 'We have to get Streaker used to travelling on long journeys in the car.' My ears went on red alert. (Although actually they're black but you know what I mean.)

'Right,' said Trevor, nodding wisely.

'So that's your job,' Mr Trevor's dad added.

'But I can't drive,' Trevor spluttered. 'I'm eleven.'

'I'm not asking you to drive, Trevor. I want you to train Streaker to sit still. That's all.'

'THAT'S ALL?! *THAT'S ALL???!!!*'

(I put those words in big black letters because Trevor shouted very loudly.)

And he went on.

'Train Streaker to sit still? That would be like training a snake to do handstands; in other words, impossible.'

Well really, do you have any idea what he meant by that, because I don't. I thought it wasn't a very nice thing to say. I'm not at all like a snake except for my tail and in fact I can do handstands but only for a tiny bit of a second. It's when I run too fast and do a somersault and there's that bit in the middle of a somersault when your legs are in the air instead of your head and your head is where your legs are. That's the handstand bit, only it's more of a paw-stand I suppose.

Trevor was pretty fed up about training me to sit still and he decided he definitely needed help so he rang Tina on his mobile and she came round at once. Tina always comes round immediately because she fancies him only he doesn't know, or at least he pretends he doesn't know. In fact Trevor is Tina's boyfriend but Tina is not Trevor's girlfriend. I think I got that the right way round. Trevor says Tina is just his friend, without the girl bit.

Excuse me while I have a good snigger because

I saw them kissing once. OK, so it was her kissing him but they were definitely kissing. She crept up on him from behind and kissed his cheek. You should have seen him jump! He rushed upstairs to the bathroom and washed his face. Three times. With soap and everything.

Anyhow, today Trevor told her about going away on holiday and that all led to another big fuss. Tina turned white and collapsed on the sofa. I thought

she'd fainted because her eyes were closed but then I saw her open one eye halfway and take a quick glance at Trevor to see if he was paying attention. Crafty, or what? It didn't do any good, though, because Trevor wasn't taking any notice.

'You're going away,' she answered in a kind of half-dead voice.

'Yes! Two weeks! In France!' (I don't think Trevor had even noticed the fainting bit.)

'I shan't see you for TWO WEEKS. I shall need trauma counselling,' murmured Tina.

Trevor just grunted. 'Don't overdo it,' he said. 'Honestly. Girls. Everything's a drama.' He sat down and folded his arms across his chest. 'You've got to help me,' he told her.

'Have I?' she answered, rather coolly, I felt.

'Please,' he added hastily.

'Maybe. What's the problem?'

Trevor explained about the training. 'After all,' he went on, 'you trained Mouse really well. He sits still, doesn't he.'

'I never taught him to do that. He's just lazy,' Tina pointed out.

Ha ha! That is so true! I've known Mouse for years. He's a huge St Bernard. You know – they're the ones that look like Shetland ponies with no neck. He's as lazy as a retired rock.

'You will send me a postcard, won't you?' Tina asked.

'I haven't gone yet,' Trevor scowled.

'I know, but I feel really weird about you going away,' said Tina. 'It feels as if we're getting a divorce.'

Trevor suddenly began coughing furiously, like a million very big words had all got jammed in his throat and he was trying to get rid of them. 'A divorce! Tina, I'm eleven! You're eleven! We're not MARRIED!'

I can tell you I was rolling on the floor. I have never seen Trevor look so horrified and embarrassed at the same time. Tina just watched him and waited until he'd finished.

'I know. It's just that . . . I shall be lonely when you're not here.'

'I'm only going away for two weeks. I'll send you a postcard, OK?'

'Only one?' Tina pulled such a miserable face I thought the furniture would start crying.

'All right, TWO postcards. Can we please train Streaker? Have you got any ideas?'

'Three.'

Trevor brightened up at once. 'Three ideas! Great!'

Tina shook her head. 'Not three ideas, you dope. Three POSTCARDS. At least three.'

'OK, OK, four postcards. I'll send you four. Now, PLEASE can we get on?'

Tina gave him a twinkly smile. 'Did you know,' she said, 'that in France, when people meet each other, they kiss on both cheeks.'

'We're not in France,' Trevor told her.

'No, but you should practise.' Tina paused. 'With me,' she added, quite unnecessarily.

Trevor leaped to his feet as if a crocodile had just bitten his you-know-what. 'I think we should try and train Streaker now. You can tell me what your idea is on the way.'

He made a grab for my lead and set off for the garden. Tina pulled the remains of a biscuit packet from her pocket and I was beside her in a flash. Biscuits are my favourite, apart from pizza, salami, ice cream, sausages, chips, roast chicken, burgers, crisps –

'You get Streaker to sit and I'll give her a bit of biscuit as a reward,' Tina said.

'Right,' agreed Trevor. 'Streaker – sit.'

– roast potatoes, doughnuts, fried onion rings, hash browns, muffins –

'STREAKER! SIT!'

– digestives, hobnobs, fig rolls, tortillas, flapjacks, cake, strawberries –

'SIT!!' Trevor tried to help by pushing my back down but my legs were carved from pure steel and my eyes were bulging with one-hundred-

per-cent biscuit
concentration.

'You're both
hopeless,' Tina
muttered impatiently.

Trevor snapped
back at her. 'Give me
the biscuits and you
get her to sit.'

Tina rolled her
eyes as if he was an
idiot with an idiot
dog and passed the
biscuits across to
him. Ha ha! They
have no idea, those
two. I was there in a
flish-flash because I
am Miss Lightning-
on-Legs. As Tina's
hand moved towards

Trevor, my mouth headed for that biscuit packet faster than a spaceship on triple warp speed. I knocked them clean from her hand.

Up they went, cartwheeling through the air. I crouched, I tensed every springy muscle in my body and – ***BOYOYOINNGG!*** – up I went, into the air and – ***SNAP, SNAFFLE, CHOMP – GONE!***

No more biscuits. I even ate the packet. Then I
sat down and looked at them both.

'Well,' Tina sighed. 'She's sitting.'

Ha ha! I love being a dog.

3 Training Trevor

Sometimes I have no idea what those two-legs
think they are doing. Mr Trevor's dad keeps
going on at him about making me sit still in the
car and then Trevor goes on at me about keeping
still in the car. What do they think I'm going to
do? I am one hundred per cent harmless.

I will sit there like a statue and not even flap
my tongue at them, or my ears. I won't even
blink, though it might be nice to sit in the front.
I hardly ever get to sit in the front because Mr
Trevor's dad won't let me and Mr Trevor's mum
only allows it when Mr Trevor's dad isn't there.
If I can't sit in the front I could try the very back
as long as there isn't too much luggage. Maybe
I could try lying on top of it. Or I could lean
against it, in an I'm-going-on-holiday kind of

pose. I bet that would look good. Or I could sit on the back seat with Trevor, as long as I'm not stuck in the middle and can't see out of the windows properly.

THE WINDOWS! I love sticking my head out so that the wind makes my ears flap like Trevor's pants on the washing line and the air goes rushing up my nostrils and I open my mouth and try to catch the wind and eat it because it tastes so fresh!

Woo-hoo! This car journey is going to be great! I can do all those things while I'm busy being still. Except, I've just thought, we won't be in the car, we'll be in a caravan. I don't know what a caravan is. Maybe it doesn't have windows. I'll ask Erik. Perhaps he knows.

Anyhow I had to have another training session today with Trevor and Tina. She was very excited because she'd had a good idea.

'Did you know, when geese are born they think the first thing they see is their mother. In the wild that's OK because their mother is the first thing they see, but in this TV programme there were some goose eggs ready to hatch but their mother had been killed by a fox. A man took the eggs home and kept them warm –'

'Did he sit on them?' Trevor asked.

Oho, that was so funny. I looked at them both, opened my mouth and howled with laughter. Trevor and Tina stared at me.

'What's wrong with her?' asked Tina.

'I have no idea.' Trevor's face was blank. 'What happened with the goose eggs?'

'They hatched out and the first thing the

goslings saw was the man, so they decided he must be their mum.'

Duh! Is that weird or what? Those baby geese must have been a bit brainless. Maybe their brains hadn't hatched out, just their goosey bits. Tina went on explaining.

'The geese followed the man wherever he went and as they grew bigger the man realized they would have to learn how to fly, but they didn't have their mother to teach them, so the man would have to show them instead.'

'But humans can't fly,' muttered Trevor, and I barked and barked and barked because I CAN FLY! I *can*! I can fly like a very flappy thing. I run and run and run until my paws aren't even touching the ground, they are just a blazing blur and I'm zooming through the air! Well, it feels like flying.

'Shut up, Streaker,' said Tina, 'I'm telling a story. So the man went up in a hang-glider and the geese all followed him, and as he took off

31

they had to flap to keep up with him – and they were flying! It was all on film. It was amazing.'

'OK,' said Trevor. 'Amazing. But how is that going to help us train Streaker? She doesn't need to learn how to fly and we don't have a hang-glider.'

Tina gave Trevor a very long-suffering look. 'You can be so dumb sometimes, Trevor.'

Ouch, I thought. *That was a bit tough!*

'Listen,' she went on. 'The geese learned how to fly by copying the man. Got that?'

'Yes.'

'So all you have to do is show Streaker how to behave so she can copy you.'

Trevor considered what Tina had just suggested. 'There are two problems,' he announced. 'Firstly, Streaker didn't hatch out of an egg, and secondly, I'm not Streaker's mum and I wasn't the first thing she saw.'

Hang on. That's three problems, not two. Trevor can't count. I told you two-legs are useless. Tina didn't notice either, so who's the clever one?

33

ME of course! I am Miss Brain-Like-a-Dog-Flap. (I said 'dog-flap' because dog-flaps are SO amazingly brilliant, aren't they? They go *flap* one way and *flap* the other way and I can go in and out without having to have doors opened. Is that clever or what? It's very, very clever and my brain is as clever as that!)

'It could still work,' said Tina. 'Let's try. Nothing else has worked, has it?'

Trevor looked at me. It was a very stern kind of look. 'Sit!' he commanded.

I thought, *Here we go again, but just for once I'll do it.* So I sat down.

Ha ha! You should have seen the pair of them. Their jaws just about fell on the floor.
KERLUNK!

'Wow!' said Trevor. 'She did it!'

'See if she does it again,' suggested Tina.

'OK. Streaker – sit!'

I thought, *Hang on, I'm already sitting, sponge-head. What am I supposed to do – get up and sit down again?*

So I shuffled about on my bottom to show them I was already sitting.

'No,' growled Trevor. 'Get up and then sit down.'

I thought, *I'm not a toy. I'm not getting up and down just because you want me to.* So I shuffled about a bit more and then they tried to make me stand up by lifting me and I went all sloppy and floppy and fell through their arms and lay on the floor and showed them my tummy so they could tickle it but they weren't interested.

'It's no good,' muttered Trevor. 'That was just a fluke.'

A fluke! Hang on, sunshine, you told me to sit and I did. Just don't expect me to do it ALL THE TIME! Anyhow, the best bit came after that because Tina told Trevor to show me how to sit and you are really not going to believe this.

TINA TURNED TREVOR INTO A DOG!

She did. Really really really!

'The thing is,' she told Trevor, 'you have to be

the dog so Streaker knows what to do.' She undid my collar and went across to Trevor. 'Put this on.'

'You're kidding me.'

'Do I look as if I'm kidding?' She fastened my collar round Trevor's neck and attached my dog lead.

'You get on all fours and follow me round the room.'

'This is ridiculous,' Trevor grumbled, but he did it. I sat there and watched as Tina led him round and round the room. I looked the other way because I thought if I watched this any longer I was going to die laughing.

'Now,' said Tina. 'Sit.'

Trevor sat back and Tina took the lead off his collar. She went to the other side of the room. 'Come here,' she said and Trevor meekly went across to her. 'Sit.' And he did. Tina patted Trevor on the head. 'Good dog.'

I'm sorry. I couldn't hold it back any longer. I howled. ***AROOOOH! AROOOOOOOOH!!***

It was SO funny!

Then Tina took the collar off Trevor and put it back on me. She attached the lead and tried to take me for a walk round the room but I just sat there. She couldn't make me budge and she couldn't make me sit either because I was already sitting.

'You'll pull her head off if you're not careful,' warned Trevor.

'I can't believe your dog is so stupid,' Tina snapped. 'Geese have smaller brains than dogs and they knew what to do.'

Ah, I thought, *that might be the case but dogs have*

bigger brains than geese and mine is the size of a dog-flap
and we are not going to be fooled by silly pretending games.
In any case, you never asked me to fly, did you? If you'd
asked me to fly I could have shown you. I would have gone
WHOOOSH! WHIZZZ! *and taken off like a jet*
fighter because I am supersonic!

So that was that.

4 Fun on the Ferry

France! We are on our way! Tina said goodbye
to Trevor – lots of tears and sniffles, boo hoo
stuff and nose blowing – all from Tina of course.
Trevor tried to pretend he wasn't there but not
very effectively because he was. He looked like an
embarrassed tomato – in other words VERY red.

'Is your girlfriend always like that when you go
away?' asked Mr Trevor's mum.

'She is NOT my girlfriend!' snapped Trevor.

'Yes, I am,' sniffed Tina, wiping her eyes again.

Mr Trevor's mum put a comforting arm round
Tina's shoulders. 'Never mind,' she said. 'One
day you'll realize there are much nicer boys than
Trevor.'

'I AM nice,' Trevor declared.

'Not to Tina, you're not,' said Mr Trevor's mum.

'But that's only because — aaargh! I can't say anything without getting it in the neck.'

Ha ha! Now Trevor knows what I feel like. I'm always getting it in the neck. Actually I don't know what that means but it sounds painful. My neck hurts just thinking about it.

I went and said goodbye to Erik but he didn't cry or sniff or anything like that. He just closed his eyes and pretended he was asleep but I knew he wasn't because I poked him and then he was awake.

'Cheerio,' I said. 'I'm going to France now.'

Do you know what he said? 'Hooray. Peace and quiet at last.' And he shut his eyes so that was that. Actually I think he's jealous. I might come back with a suntan.

Now we are on the road, zooming along and my ears are flip-flapping out of the window and we are towing a house behind us. That's what a caravan is! I have found out! It's a house on wheels and the car can pull it along.

It's fantastic! It's all shiny silver and curvy. It's got a tiny kitchen and a tiny shower and toilet and a room to sit in and eat. It's got windows and curtains and Mr Trevor's mum and dad have got a bed at the back and Trevor and I have got a bed at the front and you push a button and it goes **ERGGGGGGGG!** and slides down and out from the wall but sometimes it springs back. Trevor said it was his bed and I said it was for both of us but of course he can't understand

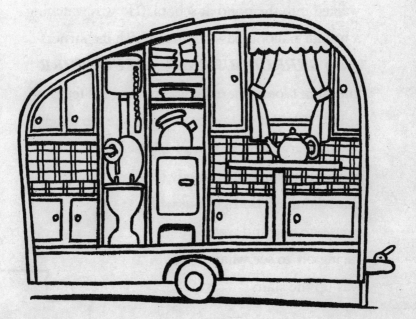

what I say but he'll soon find out. It looks very comfy if you ask me. You have to push buttons for everything. Want water? Push this button. Want to shut the curtains? Push this button. Want to push a button? Push this button. Ha ha!

I shall lie on our bed at Trevor's feet and look after him because now that Tina isn't around there's nobody else to take care of him. I shall be like his guide dog for the blind except he isn't blind but he does trip over a lot and last year he walked into the pond at school. (He was watching a hot-air balloon pass overhead with its burners going **_SKRRUUURRRR SKRRUUURRRR_** and didn't look where he was putting his feet.)

We had a bit of bother crossing the Channel on the ferry because I was supposed to stay in the car. Well, nobody told *me* that, did they? So I got out with everyone else and went racing off to see what was up the stairs and guess what? What was up the stairs was even more stairs. I was panting when I got to the top and I couldn't see where the others had got to so I went looking for them. In fact loads of two-legs were looking for them. I tried telling them where to search.

'You go that way,' I said. 'I'll go this way.'

But they kept following me, which was pretty stupid of them if you ask me, and we were rushing all over the place. Soon the crew had joined in but we couldn't see Trevor or Mr Trevor's mum and dad anywhere. Eventually I got right to the very top deck and

I saw a two-legs standing behind a big long window and I wasn't sure but it did look like Mr Trevor's dad so I barked and barked and dashed into the room where I'd seen him to say 'Found you!'

Guess what? It wasn't Mr Trevor's dad. It was a very large two-legs wearing a snazzy uniform

 with lots of gold buttons and wobbly things on his shoulders that looked like golden hairbrushes except they wobbled.

Anyhow, when Mr Gold Buttons saw me he let go of the giant steering wheel he was holding and shouted and pointed and told

me to get out so I sat down. I thought I'm not going to be spoken to like that! He didn't seem nice at all and he looked like the sort of person that might harm Trevor so I decided I should keep an eye on him. In fact I decided to keep both my eyes on him.

Mr Gold Buttons didn't like that at all and I knew that meant he knew that I knew what he was up to and he knew that I knew he knew what I was up to too. After that I felt a bit confused and before I could say '*Woof woof*' all the other two-legs came pouring into the big room and Mr Gold Buttons started shouting at everyone to get out, not just me. Then I saw Mr Trevor's mum and dad AND Trevor too. It was very strange because they were in the bunch of people that had been following me around all that time. Why didn't they say?

I was mighty pleased to see them and rushed over. Then Mr Gold Buttons started yelling and saying that he was going to throw us all

overboard. He was going to turn the ship round and take us back to England. He was going to hand us over to the French police as soon as we landed. He was going to put us all in jail.

Do you know what I told him? I said, 'Make your mind up, mate!' But of course he just thought I was barking. I keep telling you those two-legs are useless. Anyhow, I got taken back

to the car and I had to sit inside for the rest of
the voyage. Huh! Although between you and me
I can tell you I didn't sit for very long. I stood
up sometimes and once I went and sat in the
driver's seat and I rested my head on the steering
wheel only it made a terrible noise like the noise
a massive headache would make if headaches
made noises.

It only stopped when I took my head off the wheel but it took me a long time to find that out and by then several two-legs were standing outside the car hammering on the windows. They were a little bit open to let fresh air in but the two-legs couldn't get in so they just had to stand outside and shout.

Eventually we got to France without any more trouble, well not much at any rate just one or two small things like Mr Trevor's mum and dad couldn't find the sandwiches they'd brought with them for the journey. That was because I'd eaten

them when I was stuck in the car on my own.
I mean what else is a dog supposed to do? Die
of boredom? Those sandwiches had SAVED
MY LIFE!

Soon we were on the road and heading for the
campsite. I have never been camping before.
Neither have Trevor and his mum and dad. I
wonder what it will be like?

We stopped in a French town for some lunch
and I saw some French dogs. They look just like
British dogs and guess what? They speak the
same language! Brilliant. But they do have a
funny accent. Trevor once got a great Christmas

present. It was a voice changer. It was like a megaphone but when you spoke through it your voice came out all funny. French dogs sound just like that. Maybe they all got voice changers for Christmas and then ate them because I have heard that French dogs like eating even more than I do. (I bet they don't. I can't imagine anything that likes eating more than I do. I am the world's speediest speedster and eatiest eater too.)

It was so hot that Mr Trevor's dad opened up the sunroof on the car and then I put my paws on the front seat in front of me and stuck my head out of the top. *WOOO-HOOO!* It was brilliant. I could almost eat the clouds. *CHOMP! CHOMP!* I shouted at everything. I shouted at the sky and the trees and the other cars and the big trucks and the two-legs wandering about and the French dogs (and they shouted back but I couldn't hear them because we were whizzing even faster than I can run).

When I looked behind me I could see our house on wheels following and barked at that too but my ears kept getting blown across my eyes by the wind and then I fell over. My head got stuck between the two front seats just as Mr Trevor's dad went to pull on the handbrake only he grabbed my muzzle instead and clamped his fingers round my teeth and he was so surprised we nearly crashed into a hedge and guess what?

We were at the campsite!

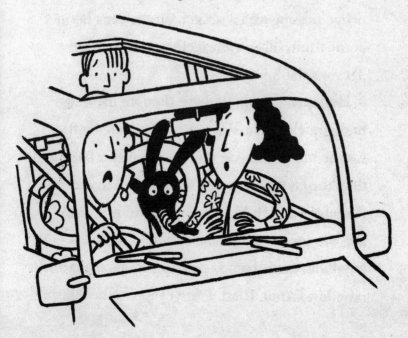

5 A Busy Day, with Saucepans and Pirates

Mr Trevor's dad kept telling everyone that I had bitten him but you know I hadn't. He shouldn't have stuffed his fingers in my mouth. Luckily there wasn't any damage done, only a bit of hedge missing and a scratch on the car's bonnet at the front. (Plus a few teeth marks on Mr Trevor's dad's hand.)

Honestly, you would have thought the hedge had scratched Mr Trevor's dad judging by the fuss he made. He yelled at me, I howled back and then the campsite owner shouted at Mr Trevor's dad and waved a big saucepan at him. I think she was threatening to cook him. They'll eat anything, those French people – frogs, snails and now Mr Trevor's dad. I don't suppose he'd taste very nice. There's too much fat on him.

The campsite owner is called Madame Crêpe and she has a daughter, Mini Crêpe. They look just like each other except one is younger. They were both wearing large sunglasses and they were big and fierce and wobbly. (I don't mean the sunglasses were fierce and wobbly, I meant Madame and Mini Crêpe.)

They shouted a lot and kept saying 'Ooh la la' and other things as if they were in a big drama, when the only thing that had happened was that their hedge had a small bruise. So there was lots of noise but it all got sorted in the end and we got a nice spot for the caravan near the river, which I immediately went and jumped in. (The river, not the spot for the caravan!)

Then I came back and told everyone they should jump in the river too because it was fabulous and I showed them how lovely it was by shaking myself really hard and showering them with water.

You can never tell what two-legs are going to do next, can you? I thought they'd be pleased and they'd all jump in the river too but they shouted at me instead so I ran off to find somebody more sensible to play with and that was when I saw –

HIM!

A vision! He was a miracle of bouncy legs and waggy tail and shiny fur and complete cuteness. What's more, he was trotting straight towards –

ME!

I stopped dead in my tracks. My legs went shaky. I felt my tongue fall out of my mouth so I put it back in and hoped he hadn't seen me looking like that. I thought, *Stay calm, Streaker, Mr Gorgeous is heading your way.* So I plonked myself on the grass and tried to look elegant and cool – one ear up and one ear down and staring at a daisy so it looked like I wasn't interested; that sort of thing.

Mr Gorgeous stopped right in front of me. I could feel his eyes watching me but I didn't look back because I thought, *If I look at him my heart will probably burst or I shall faint or do something silly like show him how to do a cartwheel.* And then he spoke. To me!

''Allo.'

His voice sent a shiver down my tail. Now I had to look at him and I lifted my head.

'Oh!' I said. I thought that was so cool of me, just pretending I didn't know he was even there! 'Who are you? Have we been introduced?'

'Ah, you English dogs, you are so reserved, so quiet.' Mr Gorgeous stretched out on the grass in front of me and tossed one ear behind his head. (I don't mean it came off; it was still attached to his head. It was just a very long, flappy kind of ear. And so was the other one.) 'Do you like it 'ere?'

'I've only just arrived,' I told him, all casual like. 'But it looks like a nice spot.'

Mr Gorgeous burst out laughing. 'Ha ha! "It looks like a nice spot!" You English, you speak so funny, as if you are about to make ze nice cup of tea and ze sandwich.'

Huh! So he was making fun of the way I spoke! Two can play at that game. 'And you French talk as if you've got a baguette stuck up your bottom!'

Do you know what Mr Gorgeous did? He laughed even more. Then I realized it was quite funny and I laughed too and soon we were both rolling about in hysterics. So after that we sat down and had a proper conversation and it turned out he wasn't called Mr Gorgeous, his name was Pascal. (But I might still call him Mr Gorgeous sometimes because he IS!)

In fact he didn't have much of a French accent because, as Pascal said, his 'muzzair' was French and his 'farzzair' was English. He wears a bright red scarf round his neck and it makes him look super cool and very, er, French.

Pascal showed me round the campsite and we chatted and chatted and it was as if we had known each other forever and I couldn't take my eyes off him. He is a proper pedigree, a bloodhound no less, whereas I'm just an ordinary mongrel.

Well, actually, I'm not so *ordinary* at all because as you know I am Miss Zippy-Paws with a Brain Like a Dog-Flap, the fastest, bravest, cleverest dog in the world. Even so, a bloodhound! It's a bit like an ordinary two-legs being introduced to a duke, or even a king.

After that I thought I had better get back to my two-legs so I said goodbye to Pascal and hoped that we would meet again and he said he hoped we would meet again too and I said let's make it soon and he said very soon and I said how about in two minutes and we both had hysterics again. I like him. A LOT!

I went trotting off to see my family and I was thinking about Mr Gorgeous Pascal and I saw another dog and he was *massive*. He was even bigger than Pascal and he had jaws like a mechanical digger. He was with two smaller dogs and they were deep in conversation. I could just about hear what they were saying because my ears can catch the tiniest sounds. I can even hear flies thinking. At least I think they're thinking. Maybe they're just brushing their teeth.

'Yeah, you know ze cars?' said the big dog.

'Yeah, we know ze cars,' said the middle dog.

'Yeah, ze cars we chase,' nodded the smallest dog.

'What about, instead of we chase zem, we jump on zem? And we bite zem and make big

teeth marks and scratch zem with our paws. Zat'd be really big funny.'

'Hurr hurr hurr,' laughed the middle dog. 'Yeah, big funny.'

'Why would zat be funny?' asked the smallest dog.

The middle dog fell silent and looked at the biggest dog. Obviously the middle one didn't know why it was funny either. The big dog snarled.

'Because it would leave ze whopping great marks on ze cars and ze people would get so angry and zey'd blame some kids or some ozzer dogs and we sit zere and watch all of it and our 'eads are laughing off.'

Then he spotted me and his ears pricked up at once. 'Ooh la la! Look at zis beauty coming our way.' The big dog got to his feet and swaggered towards me with the other two in tow.

''Ello, sweetheart,' he grinned.

'I'm not your sweetheart,' I told him. 'Are these your friends?'

'Yeah,' said the middle dog. 'We're in 'is gang. We're pirates.'

'I'm not,' said the smallest. 'I'm ze alien.'

'No, you're not. You're ze pirate,' snarled the big dog.

'I'm ze alien pirate, zen,' insisted the smallest.

'I'll deal wizz you later,' the big dog hissed and turned back to me, all teeth and smiles. 'My name,' he announced proudly, 'is Barbarossa, pirate chief.' He pointed with his nose at the middle and smallest dogs. 'He Bish, he Bosh, in my gang. You join ze gang too?'

Bish nudged Barbarossa. 'I thought we were pirates, not ze gang.'

'We're ze gang of pirates, stupid,' growled the pirate chief.

'I'm ze alien,' the small one insisted.

'I don't want to join your gang,' I told Barbarossa, while he glared at the small one. The

glare instantly snapped on to me and his lips curled back, showing his teeth. He had a lot of teeth and they all looked pretty pointy. He went on.

'If you're not in ze gang –'

'Pirate gang,' Bish butted in.

'If you're not in ze gang, we can't protect you,' Barbarossa pointed out.

'Protect me from what?' I asked.

'Ze gang,' the pirate chief declared bluntly.

Huh! We seemed to be going round in circles and I was getting dizzy. All three of them were now looking at me to see what I would do and

I thought, *Keep cool, Streaker, keep cool*.

'I'll think about it,' I said.

Barbarossa lifted his big head. 'You do zat, *cherie*,' he said. 'But you'd better zink fast. You've only got a couple of days.' He turned his back on me and called the other two. 'Come on. Let's go.'

They had barely taken a few steps when the smallest one, Bosh, trotted quickly back to me and whispered in my ear.

Do you know what he said? I will tell you. He said, 'Zey are ze pirates. I'm ze alien because I don't like boats.'

I put it small like that because he was whispering and I thought he'd finished but he suddenly stuck his snout back by my ear and went 'Grrrrr!' I think it was meant to sound menacing but it was quite sweet really, like having your ear tickled by a budgerigar.

Well, that was a bit of an adventure, wasn't it? I have a feeling I haven't seen the last of those pirates. Aliens. Whatever. What a busy day.

6 A Rather Wet Adventure

Disaster! Mr Trevor's dad's golf clubs have DISAPPEARED! They have vanished. It's almost as if they'd grown legs and run away. The whole bag has gone.

'They've been stolen,' growled Mr Trevor's dad.

Huh! Who on earth would want to steal some stupid old golf clubs? They'd have to be half mad, or even completely bonkers. Now if they'd stolen my dinner bowl that would be another matter, not that they'd ever get the chance because I would spot them and go *WOOF WOOF! RAAARRGH!* and bite their legs right off so they couldn't run away.

'I'm going to make a complaint to Madame Crêpe the campsite owner,' declared Mr Trevor's dad.

'What do you think she'll do about it?' asked Mr Trevor's mum.

He was stumped. He had no idea what Madame would do about it and neither did I but he still went off to make a complaint and Trevor went with him. When they came back Mr Trevor's dad looked just as fed up as before but Trevor was hopping about from one leg to another because he was so excited.

Mr Trevor's dad said that Madame Crêpe wouldn't talk to him because she was too busy and Trevor said yes, she was too busy because she was getting ready to canoe down the river.

'And she's taking a party of ten canoes with her and I can go because there's one canoe with nobody in it, but it has to have two people and one of them has to be an adult. Can I go? It will be brilliant!'

'I'll go!' I barked. 'I'll go with you! I like canoes. They're fantastic. What do they look like? Tell me what a canoe is! Can you eat it?'

Trevor told me to shut up, which wasn't very nice but I forgave him. 'I have to have an adult with me,' he repeated. 'Please, Dad!'

'I'm going to play golf. Ask your mother,' grunted Mr Trevor's dad.

'You can't play golf. Your clubs have disappeared. Besides, I can't swim,' she answered.

'You can, Mum. You always swim when we go to the pool at home.'

'That's because it's a pool and I can put my feet on the bottom. I can't swim in rivers.'

Huh. I didn't think Mr Trevor's mum was making any sense. I bet she *could* swim in a river. I thought I might push her in and see what happened. She looked at Mr Trevor's dad.

'You take Trevor,' she went on. 'It will help take your mind off your missing clubs.'

Trevor was beside himself.

'Dad, *please*! It will be an adventure. We take a packed lunch and everything.'

Packed lunch? This idea was sounding better

and better. I LOVE packed lunches, especially when they're un-packed. ***CHOMP CHOMP, YUM YUM.***

Eventually Dad gave in and said he'd go canoeing with Trevor and he even agreed to take me. It was barking brilliant! We had to wear lifejackets, except for me, because they didn't have one for dogs. I said it didn't matter because I can swim. I can swim like a submarine, mostly underwater. Woofy ha ha! That's a joke I just made up.

So Trevor and his dad wore lifejackets and the packed lunches were put in a blue barrel with a watertight lid and that went in the middle of the canoe. The canoes were all bright blue except for a red one. That was the leader's canoe and the leader was Madame Crêpe with her daughter, Mini.

I thought their canoe would sink when they climbed into it but it just wobbled a lot. They sat there with their big sunglasses and smiled

at everyone as if they were film stars. I think
Mini must have put on her lipstick with a large
paintbrush because her mouth looked as if it had
just had a major accident in a jam factory.

Mr Trevor's dad sat at the back of our canoe
and Trevor sat at the front. I sat on the blue
barrel so I could keep guard over the packed
lunches but I kept sliding off so I went and sat on
Mr Trevor's dad's lap and helped him by holding
the end of his paddle for him. He didn't like me
helping. I think he thought he could do better on

his own but he couldn't because he kept steering
us towards the bank.

'Streaker! Let go of my paddle! Listen, why
don't you go and help Trevor?'

I thought that was a good idea so I scrambled
up to the front and sat on Trevor's lap.

'I can't see where I'm going, Streaker! Get your
head out of the way.'

I told him I could see where we were going –
and where we were going was straight into the
red canoe with Madame and Mini Crêpe in it.

BERDANGG! SKRRRUMPPP!
SPLOOOSH!

The red canoe got a hole in it and quickly
began filling with water, with Madame and Mini
still paddling furiously. They looked SO FUNNY
but I don't think they thought it was funny at all.
They sank further and further until the water was
up to their shoulders and you couldn't see the
canoe because it had drowned but they were still
trying to paddle!

Madame Crêpe grabbed hold of the front
of our canoe trying to save herself and pulled
so hard it capsized and we tumbled into the
river and began splashing about and yelling.
(Or barking, in my case, although I was actually
saying what fun it all was.)

The other canoes paddled over to help. I tried
to scramble on board one of them but when I
got my paws on the side their canoe overturned
just like ours had and they were in the water

too. I had to go to another canoe but the people in that one shouted at me and tried to push me away with their paddles. They made their canoe rock about so much that *their* canoe tipped over so it served them right! Good thing everyone was wearing a lifejacket. (Except me, because I'm a dog and I'm the swimmiest swimmer in the world!)

Now there were nine of us thrashing around in the river, yelling and screaming. People on the bank were rushing about shouting advice. Someone threw a lifebelt into the water but it hit one of the canoes that was still afloat making a big hole and that one sank and as *they* fell in they grabbed at the canoe next to them and *that* capsized and then there were sixteen of us in the water. (I think some of the others had just jumped in to see what the water was like.)

And then – horror! I noticed all the blue barrels containing our packed lunches floating away down the river. Oh no! I knew I must

rescue them so I set off in pursuit.
I thought, *I shall be a hero for rescuing*
all the packed lunches and saving them
from a fate worse than being eaten. After
all, nobody wants to drown, not
even if you're a sandwich! I shall be
Superdog!

So off I went.

I'm not sure what happened after
that because I disappeared round a
bend, chasing after our lunches, and
I got separated from everyone. I had
to give up on the barrels eventually.
I couldn't get a grip on any of them
so I just let go and watched them
drift away, never to be seen again.

Well, not by us, anyhow. I expect there were
people further down the river who had a
fabulous time when the barrels popped up
in front of them and they opened them up
and found all those sandwiches and baguettes
and they probably ate them all and said,
'Yum yum, ooh la la, free food!' Life isn't fair
sometimes.

I dragged myself out of the water and
went back to the campsite and that's when I
discovered great excitement all over the place.

My goodness me what an argument was
going on! Madame Crêpe had managed to
find a frying pan AND a saucepan and she
was chasing Mr Trevor's dad and yelling
at him in French. I don't know what she
said but it didn't sound nice. Mini was
there too, waving a giant egg whisk and
whirring it at Trevor.

'It wasn't my fault!' yelled Mr Trevor's
dad. 'It was that pesky dog of ours! She's
always making mischief!'

Me? A mischief-maker? How *could* he say that?
After all the trouble I had been to helping him
paddle AND trying to save the sandwiches.
Nobody else tried to save them. I bet Superman
never had this kind of trouble. I should be given
a medal, not shouted at.

Then Mr Trevor's dad started on about his
golf clubs and how somebody on the campsite
had stolen them and what was Madame going
to do about that, eh? And Madame said she
couldn't care less about his stupid golf clubs and
he'd just sunk her best canoe and who was going
to get it out of the river and repair it? Besides,
that was no way to speak to a future film star.

'One day zoon I shall be ze famous person and
you will beg for mercy and my forgiveness. But
will I give it you?! Pah! *Non, non, non!*'

(I think '*non*' probably means 'no'. In any case,
they will never be film stars unless they are in a
film about big wobbly things. They had better
lose some weight.)

Meanwhile, half the other canoeists were jumping about as if their shoes were full of snapping crabs and shouting about being thrown into the river and losing their sandwiches. They all wanted their money back.

But, best of all, Trevor was suddenly a hero because while I was trying to rescue the packed lunches Trevor was busy saving a girl who was just paddling round in circles and crying. He helped her to the side and got her out of the water and her parents were massively impressed and kept saying how wonderful he was. And of course, the girl! Well! She was looking at Trevor as if he was the biggest bar of chocolate ever.

It was all terribly noisy and I didn't know what to do. I kept running around trying to decide and you'll never guess what so I will tell you. I saw Pascal again. Yes! I did. And here's another guess what. Who was Pascal looking after? Emilie, the girl Trevor had helped, and her parents! (People always seem to think that *they* look after their pets. THEY DO NOT! *We* are looking after *them*. Please remember that in future.)

Anyhow, I zoomed over to Pascal like a jet going for the world jet-speed record but then, just when I was getting near, I thought I'd better be a bit more elegant and ladylike so I slowed right down to a gallop.

Of course Pascal wanted to know what had happened and I told him everything, especially about how I had saved everyone and helped them out of the river. OK, so I exaggerated a tiny bit but only because I *would* have saved them if I hadn't been busy trying to rescue the packed lunches. One has to prioritize.

'You are so brave,' he murmured in my ear. 'Like ze princess fighting ze sea-dragon.'

That made me blush! (But I don't think he noticed, thank heavens, because I'm black all over and blushing doesn't show.)

I told him about the stolen golf clubs too and he said it was a mystery why people played golf at all and I said, 'Exactly.' We are like two peas in a pod. Except we're not green. Or small. Or round. Or edible. But you know what I mean, don't you. Then he said he thought Emilie fancied Trevor and he said 'Love is a wonderful thing,' and I said 'Yes it is and the only thing that would make it even better would be if Love was made of sausages.'

7 I Become an International Criminal!

Those thieves have struck AGAIN! This time they pinched a smart new trailer that one of the campers was using to store all their holiday gear. They also nicked a very expensive barbecue set from outside Emilie's parents' tent AND PASCAL'S DOG BOWL! How dare they!

Pascal is mortified and very upset. He says he should have heard them and if he had he would have bitten their legs off. *WOOF WOOF! RAAARGH!*

'Exactly,' I said comfortingly. 'That's what I like doing. I could have helped you. We could have had a leg each. *RAAARGH!*'

But he didn't laugh. In fact he was so

depressed I had to hold his paw and lick his ears. (Which he liked.)

Anyhow, it's not much fun having robbers running all over the campsite. What next? They might steal our wonderful caravan, the silver shell! They might kidnap Mr Trevor's dad and mum – and Trevor! Or – mega major disaster! – suppose they steal MY dog bowl!

I'll tell you what they *could* steal and it would make me very happy – Madame and Mini Crêpe. They're always complaining and telling everyone off, especially me. Just this morning they had a real go at me when all I did was eat their pizza. They shouldn't have left it on a table outside their house, should they? What a stupid place to put a pizza. The only sensible place to put a pizza is in your mouth, or rather in *my* mouth. So I did. Then they shouted at me so I shouted back.

Pascal heard me barking and came to my rescue. HE IS SO BRAVE AND HANDSOME!

He galloped right up to my side, with his great big ears going follollop-follollop.

'What is ze matter, my precious princess?'

I love the way he talks to me! I told him about the two Crêpes and he began barking at them too. That was when Madame dashed into her house and then dashed straight back out again carrying the biggest frying pan I have ever seen. It was large enough to fry a hippopotamus. Mini Crêpe followed her mother and she came whizzing back out with a giant onion in one hand and a bunch of carrots in the other. Maybe they were planning to make us into a stew.

THEY CAME CHARGING STRAIGHT TOWARDS US!

That was a bit scary, so Pascal and I took off. Madame and Mini came right after us, yelling their heads off and calling us so many names; I can't tell you what they were as I don't speak French. (I'm guessing they weren't very nice.) We shouted back at them. Then Madame Crêpe started yelling, 'Barbarossa! Barbarossa! Kill zem!'

Well, that was a surprise, I can tell you. Of course Barbarossa came crashing after us with Bish and Bosh bouncing and barking behind, ***WOOF WOOF WOOF***. It seemed like everything was shouting at Pascal and me, even the trees and the birds and the sky.

Soon most of the campers were standing outside their tents and caravans and motorhomes, watching the chase. The pirates were making enough noise to wake the dead. Yeah, yeah, we heard you, stupid pirate dogs.

Barbarossa was shouting all sorts of things at us. 'If you'd joined ze gang I could have protected you. Now I'm going to have to eat you

wiz my XXL chomping jaws and ze very sharp
teeth. I will enjoy so much.'

He said all that while he was running at full
galumph and panting so it came out even longer,
like this.

'If *(pant)* you'd *(galumph)* joined ze *(pant-pant)*

gang *(clump-clump)* I could *(pant)* have *(galumph)*
protected *(pant-pant-pant)* you,' and so on. You get
the picture.

The trouble was that there were now three dogs and two large humans after us and there were only two of us. I was fine because I can run like a wind racing another wind and winning but Pascal was not as fast because he's a bloodhound so he's slowed down by heavy things like dignity.

(Which I don't have.) Plus, he has super-giant ears that are like air breaks.

Then, to make matters worse the police-legs

arrived. (Later we discovered the police-legs were there because the people who had had their trailer stolen had called them.) I think the police-legs must like chasing people (and dogs) because that's exactly what they did. They leaped out of their blue vans, blew their whistles and came careering after us. I think they thought we were the robbers but why two dogs would want to steal a trailer I have no idea.

Anyhow, it was really difficult to get away

because they were all over the place. Everywhere
we turned someone or something got in our way.
We dashed round tents, through tents and over
tents. We slid beneath caravans and shot out the
other end. In fact we were like the most amazing
stunt dogs ever. We were!

Of course it did mean quite a few tents
got squashed, or they fell over, or they simply
collapsed altogether. In fact it was a bit like the
scene the day before with all the sinking canoes

only this time the tents were capsizing.

The people inside them weren't very happy either. They had to fight their way out and then they joined in the chase with bits of tent still stuck to them. We were being hunted down by great flapping monsters as the campers tried to free themselves from their own tents but instead just got more and more tangled up in guy ropes and cloth, not to mention arms and legs.

And then, just when I was racing along like a Ferrari with cheetah legs, there was a great big blazing barbecue RIGHT IN FRONT OF ME AND IT WAS BARBECUING!

I had to jump like the biggest jumpy thing you can think of and the barbecue was sizzling hot with flames and everything. With one giant leap I flew – see, I told you I could fly – right over the grill and I even managed to nick a sausage on the way past but it was ***OOH-OW-OOH!*** hot and I dropped it so I had to stop and grab it again.

It was quite funny really but then all of a

sudden Pascal and I found ourselves surrounded and then we were arrested. So that was that.

Madame Crêpe was fuming. She shouted at the police-legs, telling them what criminals we were. I kept trying to say it was hardly our fault. She was the one who had started everything by chasing us with frying pans and

carrots. I mean, what's a dog to do? We're not going to sit there and allow ourselves to be pelted with giant onions, are we?

Of course the police-legs just thought we were going woof woof woof. They rounded us up and we got taken to the police station along with our owners. Pascal seemed very anxious now because he'd never been to a police station in his whole life. I told him there was nothing to worry about.

'I've been arrested before,' I told him matter-of-factly. 'It's nothing, really. Just a lot of fuss.'

Pascal gave me a rather surprised look. 'You have been ze arrest before?' he asked. (I LOVE his accent!)

'Yes. Once or twice. Maybe three times.'

Pascal studied me even longer. 'Are you ze international criminal?' he asked.

That made me laugh. 'Of course not! It's just that sometimes I get into situations and –' I stopped.

This bit was going to be difficult to explain. You had to have been there really, to understand. 'I get into situations and I end up being arrested.' I gave Pascal an encouraging glance. 'You know what two-legs are like. They don't understand anything and get everything mixed up and no matter what *they* do, it's always *our* fault.'

Now THAT was something Pascal understood very well.

Madame Crêpe and Mini appeared at the police station too and made a long, long list of complaints. Honestly, I thought they'd never stop yakking. I thought we'd still be there at Christmas if they went on much longer.

Then Mr Trevor's dad got questioned and he pointed out that there were far more serious things going on at the campsite than a bit of trouble from a pair of stupid dogs.

STUPID DOGS?????!!!!!!!!!!!!!!!!!!!!!!!!!!!!!!!!!!!!!!!

I told him. I gave him an earful. I said,

'Listen here, mate. We are NOT stupid. We are super-clever, like dog-flaps. For example, I can stick my back foot in my ear. I bet you can't do that, can you? Go on. You have a go. Calling us stupid? You've got a nerve!'

But like I said before – those two-legs, they just don't listen.

Mr Trevor's dad told the police-legs they should be trying to find his stolen golf clubs, not to mention the missing trailer and Emilie's parents' barbecue stuff. Even Pascal joined in and asked what the police had done about his missing dog bowl. Meanwhile Madame Crêpe and Mini glared at everyone and huffed and puffed and folded their arms and unfolded them and folded them again.

Eventually the police-legs had to let us go with a warning. The warning was in French so I had no idea what they were saying. Pascal told me instead.

'Zey are saying if we go charging about like zat

again we shall be put in ze cages without ze key.'

I nodded and leaned against him. (I wasn't tired or anything, I just wanted to lean against him. He is such a hunk.) 'See, I told you all the police-legs do is make a fuss.'

'I zink we are in trouble,' my hero muttered, shaking his head.

I shook mine even harder. 'We haven't done anything wrong, Pascal. We weren't the only ones to have problems with tents. Barbarossa was worse than us and even the police-legs were trampling on everything.'

At that point we got separated because Pascal was put on his lead and taken off by Miss Emilie's mother. I got scooped up and shoved in our car by Mr Trevor's dad. I think his mind was on other things because he actually let me sit on the front passenger seat. Whoopee! That was a first. I sat up tall and proud and stared out of the front window, while Mr Trevor's dad got in on the other side.

A moment later there was a sharp knock on the window and Mr Trevor's dad wound it down. A police-legs loomed. He was wearing a tornado-sized frown on his face.

'I am arresting you for allowing your dog to drive ze car!' he said severely.

'My dog is not driving ze car, I mean, the car,' said Mr Trevor's dad.

'My goodness he is, oh yes, ooh la la!' said Mr Police-Legs, pointing at me.

Mr Trevor's dad looked the officer squarely in the eye. 'My dog is NOT driving the car!' he repeated. 'First of all we are not moving. Secondly, my dog cannot drive, and thirdly, this is a British car and the driving seat is on the right-hand side of the vehicle behind the steering wheel, which is where I am sitting, as you would see quite clearly if you used your eyes, you useless imbecile. My dog is sitting in the PASSENGER seat!'

I don't think anything would have happened

if Mr Trevor's dad had not used the words
'useless imbecile' to describe Mr Police-Legs.
Unfortunately he had – and we were arrested
again.

I hope we'll be let out soon.

8 We Become Ace Detectives

Poor Mr Police-Legs! The other police-legs were laughing at him for thinking I had been driving the car. He was so ashamed he let us go and we went straight back to the silver shell. When we got there I saw Barbarossa and his pirate gang waiting round the corner. They came strolling out to meet me and plonked themselves down near the silver shell as if nothing had happened, so I sat down as well. Two can play the waiting game. It's easy! So Barbarossa watched me and I watched him watching me. Yawn! Yawn!

'You run very fast,' Barbarossa eventually declared.

'I am not called Miss Zippy-Paws for nothing,' I answered.

'I haven't heard anyone call you Miss

Zippy-Paws,' observed Barbarossa.

'That's because, as I told you, I am not called Miss Zippy-Paws.' Then I laughed to show him that:

> 1. I was making a joke
>
> and
>
> 2. I was not afraid of him, or anything else, including Death. (Although I am really but don't tell anyone. I mean, Death is the end, isn't it. No more pies or sausages!)

Barbarossa was silent again. He turned and gazed at our gorgeous silver caravan. 'Ziss is where your two-legs live?'

I nodded.

'Is caravan?' he asked and I nodded again.

'It looks more like ze biscuit tin, and zat must mean you're a biscuit.'

Bish snorted. 'Yeah,' he said. 'You're a 'obnob!'

'But I'm ze alien,' insisted Bosh, who hadn't quite understood it all yet.

'Nobody asked you,' Barbarossa spat, and turned back to me. 'You should have joined ze gang,' he growled.

'I don't join gangs. Gangs are for bullies.'

Barbarossa got to his feet, growling even more. 'Are you calling me a bully?' he asked threateningly. I didn't bother to answer and eventually he sat down again.

'Zat friend of yours,' he scowled, ''e is your boyfriend?'

Ah! Now I knew what was going on. Barbarossa was jealous! *He liked me!* Aha!

'Maybe,' I said.

'I've got ze bigger teeth zan 'im,' Barbarossa declared. 'And I'm stronger.'

'Yeah,' agreed Bish. 'You know zose canoes? He bit one of zem in half last week.'

'Why?' I asked.

'Just to show I could. So I did,' Barbarossa boasted.

'I dared you, didn't I?' laughed Bish. 'I said, "I dare you to chew up zat canoe." And you did! One bite. *CHOMP!* Epic!'

'That's impressive,' I nodded. 'I guess those two-legs really need dogs that can bite canoes in half.'

'Are you trying to make me look like ze fool?' Barbarossa demanded crossly.

I smiled back at him, all innocence, and shook my head. 'I don't need to,' I said.

The pirate chief got to his feet and looked at me. 'You'd better tell your floppy-eared pal to watch out,' he warned.

'Watch out for what?' I asked.

'Zings zat bark in ze night,' Barbarossa muttered darkly. 'Let's go, pirates.'

He padded off, quickly followed by Bish. Bosh

looked at me and opened his mouth.

'I know, you're an alien,' I said quickly. Bosh gave a tiny joyful bark and skipped away quickly after the others.

Well, what a thing! Barbarossa wanted to be my boyfriend. At least I knew I was pretty safe now. I was sure that if he liked me, the pirate chief wouldn't want to hurt me, at least for the time being. On the other hand he could still do some nasty damage to Pascal.

In any case, there were other things that were more bothersome, like who was stealing all that stuff on the campsite, and what would they take next? It was time to find out and what I really needed was a bloodhound to help me – and guess what? I knew one! Lucky me! Ha ha!

It was time to turn detective. All Madame Crêpe and Mini had done so far was to huff and puff and the police-legs hadn't even bothered to come back to the campsite to do some proper searching after (wrongly!) arresting Pascal and me.

So off I trotted to see my sniffing friend. I wanted to get on with the job absolutely immediately, I was so keen. In fact I was so keen I only stopped twice on the way to Pascal's tent and that was firstly because someone had left almost a whole burger bun in the middle of the camping field, and secondly because when I hadn't even finished eating the bun I found the burger bit of it too! Was that scrumptious? It most certainly was!

When I got to Pascal's tent the first thing he said was, 'Miss Lightning-on-Legs, you have ze mustard on ze chinny-chin.'

I was rather embarrassed but not for long because I licked it off at once and it reminded me of the burger and that reminded me of the bun and that put a big smile on my face.

I told Pascal that he was a bloodhound.

'Of course. I know zat,' he told me back.

'I know you know, but listen. Bloodhounds are very good at finding things, aren't they.'

101

And Pascal nodded and he said, 'Yes, we are. Why? Have you lost something, like ze marbles?' And he started laughing so much that all the loose skin round his face shook and his ears were like big fat leaves in a gale and his laugh was like listening to ketchup gurgling down a drain. He is even handsome when he is being bonkers!

'You are a big tease,' I told him. 'I have a plan. We must find all the stolen things and it will be easy because you are a bloodhound and I can run faster than a cheetah being chased by a Ferrari being chased by a rocket being chased by something faster than a rocket.'

'But why all ze running?' asked Pascal.

'To tell everyone that we have found the thieves of course! They will want to know and when I tell them they will think we are very clever and they will pat us and say "Good doggies!" and give us medals and feed us with giant pizzas. Yum yum!'

'Hmmm. You are right about zem saying

good doggies. At ze moment zey zink we are bad
doggies. I don't like zis feeling badness. So, we
find ze treazure and everyone is happy.'

'Exactly. Come on.'

'No, first I show you zumthing,' said Pascal. He
led me over to his family's tent and peered round
the door. 'Sssh. Keep ze quiet.'

So I kept very quiet and I peeped round the
door and you will never guess what. There was
Trevor Two-Legs! I'd been wondering where
he'd got to. He was in Emilie's tent, WITH
EMILIE! They were
sitting close together
on an upturned box.
Emilie had a book
and she was
reading to
Trevor and
pointing at
something in
the book.

'What is she doing?' I whispered to Pascal.

'She is teaching him ze French,' he whispered back. 'She tells him zum French words and makes him say zem back and – look! Zat is what happens if he gets zem right!'

At that moment Emilie leaned even closer to Trevor and gave him a quick *kiss* on his cheek. SHE DID!

Trevor turned very red and tried to move a bit further away but he couldn't because he was trapped against the wall of the tent. Well, how about that! I don't know what Tina would say if she could see them. Actually, I do know what she would say but I can't tell you because your ears would probably burst into flames and you'd have to call the fire brigade to come and put them out.

Anyhow, now I knew where Trevor had been all that time. He was learning French and I'm sure he was a very good pupil. BUT – and it was a big 'but', which is why it is in big letters – Pascal and I were on the hunt for stolen goods.

We went searching high and low, in front of things, behind things, everywhere we could think of but there was no sign at all. We looked in the shed where the canoes were kept. We peeped into just about every tent, caravan and motorhome on the site, but found nothing.

Pascal was sniffing round a patch of grass. I couldn't see anything in front of him at all. He just stood there, only his head moving as he went sniff sniff sniff. I was thinking that if that was what bloodhounds were famous for, anyone could do it. I can go sniff sniff sniff – no problem.

'What are you doing?' I asked because I was getting bored with watching him do the same thing to the same patch of grass over and over again.

'I'm sniffing,' he explained. 'I smell something.'

Aha! So Pascal didn't just like sniffing grass! He was on to something. I trotted over and joined him. I took one whiff and every nerve in my nose went crazy, as if they had just arrived at the best party ever!

'Pascal! You know what that is? IT'S THE SMELL OF BARBECUED SAUSAGE!'

'Of course, my *petite champignon*! You are so clever!'

'*Petite champignon?* What on earth does that mean?'

'Little mushroom,' chuckled Pascal, and his eyes twinkled.

I thought, *Maybe this French bloodhound is going mad*, but Pascal was already on the trail, nose to the ground. I trotted after him in an admiring kind of way. He is so clever. And handsome. Have I told you that before? Well he is.

At last we reached a high hedge and followed it round until we came to some big wooden gates. That was where the sausage trail ended. The gates were padlocked of course and there was no way we could get in.

'Let's go back to the hedge and see if we can squeeze underneath,' I suggested.

'A good idea, my *petite chou-fleur*.'

My heart sank. What was it going to be this time? 'And what does "*petite chou-fleur*" mean?' I asked.

'Little cauliflower.'

'I'm not a little cauliflower or a mushroom!' I shouted and Pascal just grinned at me.

'It is a term of affection,' he said quietly.

Huh! Little cauliflower indeed! I shall tell
him he's a big fat cabbage. I think he's got
vegetables on the brain. Anyway, I found a bit
of space under the hedge and I thought I could
squeeze through and I did but Pascal couldn't
because he's bigger than me and more solid and
his enormous ears kept getting caught on the
branches.

'You stay there then,' I said. 'I'll hunt around
and report back.'

'Be careful, little cauliflower,' he murmured
and I heard the ketchup gurgle down the drain
again.

Well, I had hardly started to look around when
guess what I saw? The trailer! And next to it
was the barbecue set! I couldn't see Mr Trevor's
dad's golf bag anywhere or Pascal's dog bowl
but maybe they were in the trailer. Then I tried
to work out where I was on the campsite and
you will never guess where I was, not in a million
years, so I will tell you.

9 Buckets of Water and Other Shocking Behaviour

I was in Madame Crêpe's back garden! That was a surprise, I can tell you. I couldn't have been more surprised if a van full of pies had exploded right in front of my nose and all the pies had come zooming straight into my mouth. ***CHOMP CHOMP, YUM YUM!***

I was still in a state of shock and surprise when Mini Crêpe came out of the house and saw me.

'Ooh la la! Zat 'orrible dog is in ze garden, *Maman*!' she yelled.

I looked all around for the horrible dog but I couldn't see one anywhere. Then I realized that Mini Crêpe was talking about me! *ME!! A horrible dog?* I don't think so! I told her straight up. I said, 'Listen, mate, if anyone's horrible around here it is YOU and your mother, always shouting at everyone, bossing us about, telling us what to do. And I'm not even talking about the frying pans and carrots even though I just have.'

I was going on at her like that when Madame herself came bursting out of the house, not to mention her apron, waving half her kitchen at me again. I think she must have a thing about saucepans and suchlike. Not only that but Barbarossa came charging out with her. I might have known!

He didn't even stop to say hello. He came

straight for me, barking his head off and jaws
wide open. He could swallow an elephant with
a mouth that big. I knew he liked me but you
can go off people and I wasn't going to take any
chances with those great fangs of his. I zipped
back to the hedge and slipped beneath it.

A moment later I heard a crash and a startled
yelp as Barbarossa careered into it. This was
followed by a scream of rage from Madame
Crêpe and a large saucepan came whizzing over
the top of the hedge before bouncing harmlessly
down the field in front of us.

I expected Barbarossa to slip beneath the hedge at any moment but he didn't. Maybe he was too big. Anyhow, Pascal took one look at me and understood the situation.

'Trouble,' he grunted and I nodded. We hightailed it as far as the campsite's play area and hid beneath the big log-climbing pyramid. Pascal flopped down on the ground and frowned at me.

'Spill ze beans,' he growled.

'What beans?' I asked. 'I don't have any beans. Besides I'm getting fed up with all these vegetables. First of all it was mushrooms, then cauliflowers and now beans.'

'Princess,' he smiled, 'when I said spill ze beans I meant tell me everyzing.'

I told him all about the trailer, the barbecue set, Barbarossa and the house.

'So, Madame Crêpe iz ze rubber,' Pascal muttered grimly.

'She's a rubber?' I repeated. 'What is she rubbing?'

'She rubbed ze trailer and ze barbecue and –'

Light dawned. Bulbs flashed. 'Ah! You mean *robber*! Yes, yes, you are quite right, my ginormous, hunky cabbage. Madame and her daughter are the thieves! Now we must tell everyone and this time the police-legs can arrest *them*!'

Then I told him he was so clever to track the barbecued sausage smell to the garden and he said I was so brave to go under the hedge and face the dragons. 'Like ze real princess,' he added and I felt my eyes turn into stars and my heart almost burst but I'm glad it didn't.

We emerged carefully from the log pyramid. Luckily there was no sign of Madame or Barbarossa and his gang. We made our way to the silver shell only to find Mr Trevor's mum and dad on their way out.

'Where have you been?' demanded Mr Trevor's dad. 'We've been hunting for you all over the place!'

I sat there and said it was a pity he hadn't hunted in Madame Crêpe's garden because then he might have found his stolen golf clubs. Of course he didn't understand a word or a woof I said. Those two-legs really are the most useless things in the History of Nature. In fact, if there was a Museum of Stupidity those two-legs would be the biggest exhibit of all.

'We are going out,' said Mr Trevor's dad. 'We're going into town to get some food. Trevor is on the water chute with Emilie. We won't be long. Make sure you behave yourselves.'

I looked at him. Behave myself? What did he think I was? Some kind of super-criminal-hooligan kind of dog? I was shocked. I looked at Pascal and said, 'See what I have to put up with?'

Pascal nodded wisely. He is such a support. Anyway, we had to stop them from going so Pascal stretched himself in front of the caravan door so Mr and Mrs would have to climb over him if they wanted to go anywhere at all and

I told them everything I knew about Madame Crêpe and the stolen equipment.

'So you must call the police-legs and tell them and then they can come to the campsite and arrest Madame and Mini and put them in jail,' I explained.

That was when Mr Trevor's mum threw a bucket of water at us, including the bucket. It landed on my head and everything went dark and I couldn't see. All I heard was a lot of scuffling

and Pascal moaning and then it went quiet. By the time I got the bucket off my head Mr and Mrs had gone and all that was left was a large puddle on the caravan floor and an even larger mountain of wet brown fur sitting outside and looking very sorry for itself.

'I'm wet,' Pascal said, as if I hadn't noticed. He got to his feet and gave himself a shake. Have you ever been in a monsoon? I hadn't either until Pascal shook himself dry. Now we were both soaked.

I was about to complain when Trevor and Emilie appeared. They were wearing their swimming cozzies and had towels wrapped round them. He was wearing a face like thunder and she was trotting happily at his side trying to hold his hand. Sweet!

'What have you two been doing?' demanded Trevor. 'Having a water fight?'

I could have asked him the same question since we all seemed to be wet. They came into

116

the caravan to dry off and we followed them in and I tried to explain about Madame Crêpe all over again. I even did my very best ear-semaphore signalling but Trevor was just being dense and didn't understand a woof I said.

He went into the little kitchen to make some sandwiches or something because Emilie said she was hungry. I said I was hungry too and Pascal said he was hungry but Trevor didn't bother to make either of us sandwiches. Typical. He just ignored us. We could have been invisible.

The caravan door banged shut and I thought it was the wind but it wasn't because then the caravan gave a little rock as if a mini-earthquake had taken place and just as we were all looking at each other and wondering what was happening, the caravan began to move! It did!

In fact it wasn't just moving, it was travelling. Hey, we were being towed out of the caravan park. Someone was towing us and it certainly wasn't Mr Trevor's mum and dad because they'd gone to town in their car!

Trevor scrambled to the window at the front of the caravan. He stared out and then turned back and looked at us with a face as white as a bowl of milk with a hole at the bottom.

'It's Madame Crêpe!' he cried. 'She's stealing the caravan and we're being kidnapped!'

10 It All Gets Terribly Exciting!

Trevor was right. Madame Crêpe was
stealing the silver shell! Maybe she
didn't know we were inside but the
fact was that we were. Now the silver
shell was bucketing about and we
were slippy-sliding all over the place.
Nothing had been put away so plastic
plates came whizzing off the table and
skittered across the floor. Pans fell off
the cooker. The wardrobe door banged
open and vomited shirts and skirts and
socks and shorts and underpants across
the room.

Pascal had
spreadeagled
himself on the floor in
an effort to stay in one place.
It didn't work. As we hurtled round
corners he slid everywhere like a strange furry
plane that had crash-landed. Inside a caravan.

'Do something, Trevor!' Emilie cried. 'You
must save us!'

And I thought, *Yes, Trevor Two-Legs. Save us. Do
something. That would be a good idea.*

And then he did.

'My mobile!' he shouted. 'Quick, Emilie,
what's the emergency number in France?'

'One-One-Two! No, wait, One-Two-Three!
One-Two-Two! Two-One-One! I DON'T
KNOW! I CAN'T REMEMBER!'

Huh!
Girls are
useless. Hang on, I'm
a girl. So we're not so useless
after all. In fact I am very clever. Not
only can I stick my back paws in my ears,
I can eat ice cream and roast beef at the same
time! Aha! I bet you couldn't do that.

'I think you were right the first time,' said
Trevor Two-Legs. 'I'll call one-one-two.'

It worked!

'Police? Can you understand English? You can?
Ooh la la! We are prisoners in a stolen caravan.
We are being kidnapped from our campsite.
No, I don't know where we are. If I look out of
the window I can see we are following the river.
Which side of the river? The left-hand side.
Please come quickly. Whoa!' (That was when we
went whizzing round a sharp bend and Trevor
was thrown on to the sofa.) 'How many? There
are two of us.'

My ears went on red alert, I can tell you. '*Two
of us?*' I told him. I said, 'Listen, mate, there
are *four* of us in this speedy house on wheels.
We might be dogs but we are just as important
as you are. If it hadn't been for us the stolen
property would never have been discovered. In
fact if it hadn't been for us making that discovery
then Madame Crêpe probably wouldn't have

stolen the silver shell and we wouldn't be in the dreadfully dangerous situation that we are in right now. In fact put like that it's all OUR fault.'

Oh dear. I should have kept quiet, shouldn't I.

It didn't matter anyway because Trevor had no idea what I was woofing on about.

He was far too busy phoning his parents and telling them what was going on. 'Dad, stop shouting at me and listen. It's not our fault. Madame Crêpe has stolen the silver shell. I've already told the police. YES, OF COURSE I'LL TELL MADAME CRÊPE NOT TO SCRATCH THE CARAVAN! NO, DAD, I DON'T KNOW IF MADAME HAS GOT YOUR GOLF CLUBS WITH HER. JUST COME AND SAVE US. PLEEEEEASE!'

We were really speeding along now. We had managed to squeeze ourselves into tight places where we could hold on to something. My teeth were firmly gripped round a table leg. Even so, sometimes I was under the table and sometimes I was swooshing out around it, polishing the floor with my tail.

At last, in the distance we could hear police sirens. Wee-woo, wee-woo! They were getting nearer and nearer. Trevor rushed to the back window.

'I can't see them yet!' he yelled. 'They're still some way off. I bet Madame Crêpe must have heard them.'

He was right too. The silver shell began to slow down. Madame Crêpe was coming to a stop! We were saved! Trevor was back at the front window, watching, as Madame pulled over to the side of the road.

She leaped out, raced round to the back of the car, unhitched the caravan, whizzed back to her car and took off again – without us! She was making a run for it!

Emilie threw herself into Trevor's arms. 'You saved us!' she cried. 'You saved my life – AGAIN! You are so brave! And so 'andsome!'

Hang on a minute, I thought, *that's what I say about Pascal. He's brave and handsome, although he isn't quite so brave and handsome at the moment because he's just been sick on the caravan floor. It must have been all those bendy roads and all that bouncing. I shall probably have to hold his paw and lick his ears again.*

Just as we were all thinking *Whoopee, we're saved*, the caravan began to move again, ALL BY ITSELF! It wasn't being pushed and it wasn't being pulled. It was simply rolling downhill – STRAIGHT TOWARDS THE RIVER!

'We must jump out!' Trevor cried.

'We're going too fast!' sobbed Emilie. 'We're going to die − and get wet!'

Then everything went higgledy-piggledy-bounce and there was an enormous **SPLOSH!** and a moment later we were being carried away by the river. The silver shell was afloat, but look! Water was coming in under the door.

The police sirens were right beside us now and we could see them racing along the road

and there were Mr Trevor's mum and dad too, and Emilie's parents, all in their cars, bouncing along the river bank, waving and shouting at us.

Two police cars went speeding ahead. Mr Trevor's dad was bellowing at us from his car. 'They're going to throw a rope for you! Hang on to it and we can pull you to safety. The rapids are just ahead. You don't want to get caught up in them. The caravan might get scratched!'

Looking out of the front window of the caravan, we could see the police-legs up ahead, waiting to throw a life-saving rope to us. Trevor balanced on the table and opened the roof hatch so he could stretch out and catch it but when Mr Police-Legs threw the rope it missed by miles and simply fell into the water.

'We're going to drown!' Emilie sobbed and I thought *If she cries much more we'll drown from her tears, let alone the river.* Mind you I wasn't exactly happy. My heart was in my throat. Then I realized that with all the bobbing about on the river it was actually Pascal's back foot that had got jammed under my chin.

Now we were coming to a bridge where the road crossed the river and the rapids began. I stared in utter astonishment. My eyes almost popped out of their sockets. You will never guess who was standing on the bridge parapet.

?????

There, see, you couldn't guess, could you. I will

128

have to tell you. It was Barbarossa and Bish and Bosh the alien.

What on earth
were they doing there?
Just as the silver shell was
about to go swooshing beneath the
bridge I saw Barbarossa leap into
the air with a single gigantic bound.

My goodness, if he'd had a cape he
would have been just like Superman but without
the red underpants.

There was a loud thump on the roof as he
landed and skidded about. A moment later his
big head was pushing through the roof hatch

129

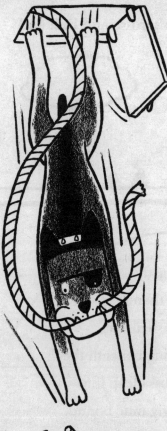

and then he came
tumbling in WITH
THE END OF A
ROPE CLASPED IN
HIS JAWS!

HUGE WOOFY
APPLAUSE!! HIP
HIP WOOFAY!!!

In a trice Trevor
had tied the rope
round the table,
the one that I had
been gripping with
my teeth. The slack
ran out, the rope
went taut, there was
a terrible jerk as
it tightened and a
dreadful ripping noise
as the table was torn
completely from the

floor. It went whizzing up through the air but was too big to go through the ceiling flap and so it jammed tight.

We weren't going any further down the river. The rope held. The police-legs tied the other end to one of their cars and slowly, bit by bit, we were pulled back to the bank and out of the river. We were SAVED!

I jumped on to solid ground. Phew! I went straight across to Barbarossa. 'You were – extraordinary,' I told him. 'You're a hero.'

'I prefer being ze pirate,' he growled.

'Yeah, we're ze pirates,' said Bish.

'I'm –' Bosh began.

'Shut up!' we chorused.

'But why did you save us?' I asked.

The pirate chief studied his paws while he thought. 'It was exciting,' he said in a low voice. 'And I . . . like you. I didn't want anyone to get 'urt.'

'But you almost ate me when you chased me

from Madame Crêpe's garden. You had all your teeth showing and you were slavering like a werewolf.'

'I wasn't going to eat you. Madame was zere. I 'ad to make it look like I was ze fierce monster.'

'But you're in a gang,' I pointed out.

'Ze pirate gang,' put in Bish.

'Shush,' Barbarossa and I snapped back, and he did. Barbarossa shrugged and went on. 'I was bored. Nothing to do all day. Zen my mistress, Madame, she start stealing things and it goes more exciting. I zought I could do zumthing like zat so I make pirate. Zen you arrived on ze campsite and everyzing change because you're so – different. ANNOYINGLY different! I was *trying* to make my life exciting, but you, you are exciting. Zat's how I want to be.'

I looked at Barbarossa. He was quite cute really. All he wanted was something to do. I felt I should show him how grateful I was for

saving us all, so I bit his ear and said he was
a cauliflower but he just looked puzzled. Very
puzzled.

11 Croissants! Baguettes! Postcards!

All around us the two-legs were patting each other on the back and yakking frantically at each other the way they do when there's a bit of drama going on and then it's all over. They talk about it. For *hours*. I just go to sleep. Trevor and Emilie were checked over and found to be shaken and a bit damp but otherwise all right.

'Trevor saved us,' Emilie said, clinging to her hero. 'He was amazing.'

'He's a star,' said all the big two-legs, even the police, but they said it in French. Pascal told me.

'Actually,' I felt I had to point out, 'it was Barbarossa who saved us. He risked his life to jump on to a sinking caravan.'

'Be quiet, Streaker,' ordered Mr Trevor's dad.

Which just goes to show how ungrateful those two-legs can be sometimes.

A police van turned up and guess who they had inside? Madame Crêpe and Mini. Their car had been stopped at a roadblock further on. It turned out that Madame and Mini had been planning to sell all the stolen equipment so that they could have some plastic surgery done.

'All we wanted was to look like ze film stars,' wept Madame. 'We wanted to go to 'ollywood and sweep down ze red carpet with everyone staring at us and saying, "Ooh la la, zey are so beautiful, I wish I was like zem." Now zat will never 'appen.'

Madame seemed quite harmless without her big frying pan. Mini was beside herself. 'My dreams 'ave been shattered,' she dribbled through her tears. 'I was planning to take 'ollywood by storm.'

I looked at all of them and sighed. They're such messy things, those two-legs. They make everything in life so complicated when it's really very simple. They're always dreaming of being something else. Why can't they just be themselves? Like me!

You don't need to be beautiful to be happy. You don't need to be a film star or famous or important or anything like that. All you need are a few sausages. Or pies. Or pizzas. Burgers. Ice cream. Roast chicken. Kebabs.

That's what I think.

Anyway, the silver shell got towed back to the campsite. It wasn't too badly knocked about, just the odd dent here and there and guess what? There was a red canoe stuck underneath it. There was! It must have got caught up in the caravan wheels when we were floating down the river. Mr Trevor's dad gave it back to Madame, who had been taken to the campsite by the police to show them all the stolen goods in her garden.

'You wanted your canoe back,' he told her. 'Here it is.'

Madame Crêpe gazed at all the holes in it and said it looked more like a watering can than a canoe so maybe she'd grow some runner beans in it.

'I didn't know zere was anyone in ze caravan when I took it,' she confessed. 'I would never have taken it if I'd known. Of course, if it had just been ze dogs –'

I never heard what she said next because Pascal put his paws over my ears in case I was offended. He's thoughtful like that.

In the end the police-legs decided they wouldn't send Madame and Mini Crêpe to jail because everyone had got their stolen things back. The police-legs even found Pascal's dog bowl but they never worked out how it had got there and Pascal and I were keeping quiet. We owed the pirate chief.

So instead of going to jail, the police-legs ordered Madame and Mini to offer an apology to the campers by cooking a huge feast for everyone except themselves – because the police-legs had also put Madame Crêpe and Mini on a special diet of beans and cauliflower. Woofy ha ha! (Except that they had the last laugh because the vegetables made them both HIGHLY EXPLOSIVE!)

So everything came out right except that the two-legs were so busy congratulating themselves they forgot all about us dogs.

So I told them.

I said, 'Just a minute, mateys. Barbarossa should get a medal for being so brave and saving us, and Pascal and I should get medals too because we discovered the stolen things and who the thieves were.'

And did we get medals? Of course not. Instead, Mr Trevor's mum told me to be quiet and to stop interrupting everyone and would I ever learn to keep my mouth shut? Well that wasn't very nice, was it? I don't know why we bother hanging around with two-legs at all and we probably wouldn't if they weren't quite so good at cooking.

A couple of days later it was the end of our holiday and we had to say goodbye to the campsite and that meant saying goodbye to

Barbarossa and Pascal too. That was sad,
especially for Pascal and me.

'I shall never forget you,' I said. 'You must
come to Britain some time.'

'Maybe you will return next year?' Pascal
suggested and I smiled and nodded because
maybe I will but of course I don't know what's
going to happen from one minute to the next
in my life. I mean one minute I'm almost being
barbecued and the next I'm in a caravan floating
down the river. And of course there was all that
business over being jabbed with the Eiffel Tower.

I'm not sure I want to go through that again unless Trevor Two-Legs has got some more jam doughnuts.

Then I saw Barbarossa standing away from everyone a little bit, with his gang of two. I trotted over to say farewell. He told me I was the most wonderful dog he had ever met.

'You're nice too,' I told him because he was. 'You were a great pirate.'

'So was I,' said Bish.

'I was ze alien,' Bosh pointed out for the last time.

'You were certainly on anozzer planet,' grunted Barbarossa and that made us all laugh.

I have no idea what things will be like when we get home. I think Trevor Two-Legs might have a few problems. Do you know how many postcards he sent Tina while he was in France? NONE. He's going to have fun explaining that one to Tina. Not to mention Emilie, who kissed him goodbye and told him she would come and see him. In Britain.

As for Mr Trevor's dad, he didn't manage to get one single game of golf all the time we were there. Poor man. Maybe we shall have to come back to France and the campsite after all. Croissants! Baguettes! French sausage! *CHOMP CHOMP, YUM YUM!*

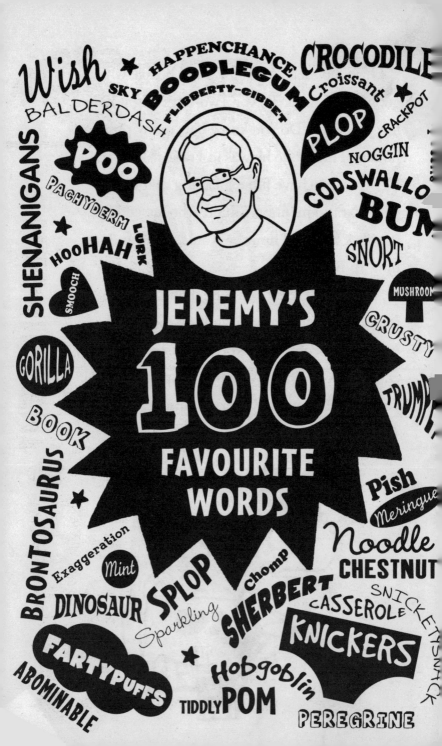

LAUGH YOUR Socks off with Jeremy STRONG

Jeremy Strong has written SO many books to make you laugh your socks right off. There are the Streaker books and the Famous Bottom books and the Pyjamas books and . . . PHEW!

Welcome to the JEREMY STRONG FAMILY TREE, which shows you all of Jeremy's brilliant books in one easy-to-follow-while-laughing-your-socks-off way!

MY BROTHER'S FAMOUS BOTTOM
Nicholas's baby brother, Cheese, is famous. Well, his bottom is, because he advertises Dumper disposable nappies . . .

It all started with a Scarecrow

Puffin is over seventy years old.
Sounds ancient, doesn't it? But Puffin has never been
so lively. We're always on the lookout for the next big
idea, which is how it began all those years ago.

Penguin Books was a big idea from the mind of
a man called Allen Lane, who in 1935 invented
the quality paperback and changed the world.
**And from great Penguins, great Puffins grew,
changing the face of children's books forever.**

The first four Puffin Picture Books were hatched in 1940 and the
first Puffin story book featured a man with broomstick arms called
Worzel Gummidge. In 1967 Kaye Webb, Puffin Editor, started the
Puffin Club, promising to **'make children into readers'**.
She kept that promise and over 200,000 children became devoted
Puffineers through their quarterly instalments of *Puffin Post*.

Many years from now, we hope you'll look back and
remember Puffin with a smile. **No matter what your age
or what you're into, there's a Puffin for everyone.**
The possibilities are endless, but one thing is for sure:
whether it's a picture book or a paperback, a sticker book
or a hardback, **if it's got that little Puffin
on it – it's bound to be good.**